Dear Parents:

Even at a very early age, children understand that police officers play an important role in their community. Young children see police officers directing traffic, at the scene of car accidents, and at events with large crowds. Children look up to police officers and often want to become one when they grow up.

Helping children understand a typical day in the life a police officer is one of the objectives of this book. We want all children to know they can turn to an officer for help, especially in an emergency situation.

We are pleased that this book helps children understand that the police serve to protect even the youngest members of the community.

Sincerely,

Bruce D. Glasscock
Chief of Police, Plano, Texas

Art Director: Tricia Legault
Designer: Nelson Greenfield

Special thanks to the Plano, Texas Police Department and the 1997 Plano Balloon Festival. And a special thank you to Detective Michael Johnson for his invaluable contribution and commitment to this book.

Printed at ColorDynamics, Allen, Texas 75002

Distributed in the U.S. by Lyrick Publishing.

1 2 3 4 5 6 7 8 9 10   00 99 98
ISBN 1-57064-238-9

Library of Congress Number 97-72911

Barney & BJ Go To The Police Station

Written by Mark S. Bernthal
Photography by Dennis Full

Officer Tom talks about safety at scho

"I want to be a police officer when I grow up, Barney!" says BJ.

"Okay! Then let's visit my friends at th police station," replies Barney.

Barney introduces BJ to his friend, Officer Mike.

"Welcome to the police station," says Officer Mike. "I'll show you around!"

"What's happening here?" asks BJ.

"These new police officers are promising to protect and help everyone," explains Officer Mike.

"Police officers help us in lots of ways," explains Officer Mike. "Sometimes they direct traffic around an accident..."

"...or ride a horse and show people where to go."

"Some officers ride bicycles..."

"...while others ride fast motorcycles."

"Vroom! Vroom!" shouts BJ.

"This is our dispatch area," explains Officer Mike. "A dispatcher tells police officers where to find people who need them."

"Look at all those screens," says BJ. "And check out that big map!"

"That dog is a police officer, too!" exclaims Barney.

"Yes," says Officer Mike. "He's specially trained to find people or things by his sense of smell. He also protects police officers. But we shouldn't pet him while he's working."

"Sometimes we use fingerprints to identify people," says Officer Mike, holding up an identification card.

"It's pretty easy to tell which print is mine!" chuckles Barney.

"Hey, where did BJ go?" wonders Officer Mike.

"I like your badge, Officer Mike," says BJ. "Your uniform is cool, too!"

"Thanks," answers Officer Mike. "You know, BJ, a gun is a part of a police officer's uniform, but they aren't toys to play with. If you ever see a gun, don't touch it and go tell a grown-up."

Badge

Radio

Beeper

Handcuffs

Flashlight

Gun

Sam Browne Belt

"This computer screen tells me where I'm needed, and I talk to the dispatcher on this microphone," explains Officer Mike. Just then, he hears his number called on the police radio.

"Uh oh! Gotta go! Someone needs my help!"
says Officer Mike, as he buckles up his seatbelt.
"See you soon, Barney. Thanks for visiting, BJ!"

"Thank you, Officer Mike!" says BJ.

"When I grow up, I want to be a police officer so I can help people," says BJ.

"That's super-dee-duper!" agrees Barney.